KU-827-108

For the Conways
of Elvan Lodge

First published 1988 by Walker Books Ltd
87 Vauxhall Walk, London SE11 5HJ

This edition published 2005

© 1988, 1992 Colin McNaughton

The right of Colin McNaughton to be identified as
author of this work has been asserted by him in accordance
with the Copyright, Designs and Patents Act 1988

This book has been typeset in Plantin

Printed and bound in Great Britain by J.H. Haynes & Co. Ltd

All rights reserved. No part of this book may be reproduced,
transmitted or stored in an information retrieval system in any form
or by any means, graphic, electronic or mechanical, including
photocopying, taping and recording, without prior written
permission from the publisher.

British Library Cataloguing in Publication Data:
a catalogue record for this book is available from the British Library

ISBN 1-84428-601-0

www.walkerbooks.co.uk

COLIN McNAUGHTON

JOLLY ROGER

AND THE PIRATES OF CAPTAIN ABDUL

WALKER BOOKS

AND SUBSIDIARIES

LONDON · BOSTON · SYDNEY · AUCKLAND

CONTENTS

SELLY OAK LIBRARY

BIRMINGHAM LIBRARIES

11/05

J

CHARACTERS

This is Roger, our hero.

This is Roger's mum.

Her name is Ernestine.

Sourpuss!

Miseryguts!

Grump!

Grouch!

PART I
Roger's Lot

"RATS!" cursed Roger as he walked down to the shop in the port where he lived. "I'm fed up!"

"Mornin', Jolly Roger," said a passing youth. "What are you looking so grumpy about? Lost a shilling and found a penny, eh? Ha ha!"

Everyone called Roger "Jolly Roger" because he always looked so miserable.

The reason that Roger and his mum were so miserable was all because Roger's dad had disappeared when Roger was just a baby.

His dad had last been seen talking to
some pirates in an inn on the coast of
Africa. When his ship returned,
Roger's dad was not on it.

Roger's mum
had never
smiled again.

Pirates?

Pirates!

Roger was turning
all this over in his
mind when he
reached the
grocery shop.
Taped to the window
was a poster.

Pirates!

10

Joyn The Pirates

—Cabin Boy Rekwired
Fool Traynin Givin.
Hoper Toon Hity 4 Travil

Gud Promoshun Prospex

No Softees Kneed Apply

See Abdul the Skinhead
Captin of the GOLDEN
BEHIND   his mark   Oooh-arrgh!

"That's it!" shouted Roger. "I'll join the pirates and run away to sea! Maybe I'll find my dad! And when I grow up and I'm all huge and hairy, I'll come home and say 'Ha!' to my mum. 'Take that, and that!'"

While Roger was pretending to slice up
his mum like a salami, he failed to notice
the pack of horrible, hairy, dirty, smelly,
ugly, scary men creeping up on him.

Take
that!

Without so much as a "How do you
do" they stuffed young Roger into a sack!
   "'E'll do!" they shouted. "Just the right
size for a cabin boy! Let's get 'im back
to the ship."

PART II
Kidnapped! Oooh-arrgh!

When Roger was tipped
out of the sack, he found
himself surrounded
by pirates. All of them,
he noted, had bits
missing – fingers, eyes, ears, even legs!

"Belay below thar, me wee
barnacle! Ha-har! Oooh-arrgh!"
bellowed a great big
hairy brute.

Must be the captain, thought Roger.
He's got more bits missing
than anybody else.

"Oooh-arrgh!" howled the captain again. "What be that 'orrible rotten smell, eh? Be that ye a-stinkin', landlubber? Pooh, it's disgustible!"

"I'm sorry," said Roger, "but can't you speak English?"

"HINGLISH!!!" stormed the captain. "Shiver me tonsils and avast me wooden leg! A-course I speaks the Hinglish, yer cheeky wee fish hook!"

(All pirates at this time in history spoke in this funny way. No one is sure why. Maybe it was because they were all extremely thick!)

"Well, you didn't have to press-gang me," said Roger. "I was just about to apply for the job anyway!"

"Oh," said the captain. "Well, what is that horrible pong a-waftin' across me poop deck?"

"It'll be the smell of soap, Cap'n!" said one of the pirates. "It's the wee lad there. He stinks of it!"

All the pirates cried:

"POOH!"

"YUK!" and

"PASS ME A CLOTHES-PEG BEFORE I'M SICK!"

"So," said the captain, "yer wants ter be a pirate, eh, soapy chops? What's yer name?"

"It's Roger,"
said Roger.

"That's a useless
name for a
pirate," scoffed
the captain.
"If yer wants to
be a real pirate,
yer needs a nickname.
Oooh-arrgh!"

"What sort of nickname?" asked
Roger rather sulkily.

"Come on me hearties!" bellowed
the captain. "Let's show him some real
pirate nicknames! Oooh-arrgh! Sing him
yer songs!"

19

21

"I suppose I do have a nickname,"
said Roger. "Because I look so miserable,
folks call me Jolly Roger!"

"JOLLY ROGER!" roared the pirates.
"That be perfeck! Oooh-arrgh! That's
what we calls our flag – the Jolly Roger!"

"SHUT YER GOBS!" bawled Captain
Abdul. "Let the lad speak. I wants to
hear what makes him so grouchy."

"Well," said Roger, "it's my mum. She's the cleanest, tidiest, grumpiest person in the whole world. Every day I've got to make the beds, get washed, comb my hair, brush my teeth, do the dishes, bake the bread, scrub the floors, clean the pigsty, wash the cow, polish the goat, shampoo the chicken, whitewash the coal – on and on and on!"

What's a comb?

On and on and on.

(Well it was almost true, thought Roger, crossing his fingers.)

"Poor wee scab!" growled the captain. "It ain't right for a lad to be brought up so clean!

26

"NO! Kids should be smelly an'
'orrible. It's the only chance they gets
before they grow up into people!
Unless they become pirates! Then they
can be dirty, smelly, lazy an' 'orrible all
their lives! Ya-har! Ain't that the truth,
me hearties, eh? Oooh-arrgh!…

"What do you say, me lads?
Should we go an' teach
his mum a lesson?
Should we go an'
shiver her timbers?"
"AYE!" roared the crew.
"LET'S GO GET HER!"

The pirates swarmed into the rowing boat, leaving only Roger and the cook behind.

"Cookee!" yelled the captain. "Give the lad some grub – he needs buildin' up if he's goin' ter be a pirate. Oooh-arrgh!"

Roger wanted to call out not to hurt his mum, but it was too late. The pirates were already speeding towards the quay – the captain water-skiing behind.

Cookee gave Roger a huge plate
of sausages and beans smothered in
chocolate sauce and chopped bananas.
It was delicious!

"Cookee," said Roger, "why didn't
you have a song?"

"Oh, that's because I'm not a proper
pirate. I do have a little song of my own
but it's not a pirate song. You see, when
I was press-ganged like you, they bopped
me on the head and I lost my memory.
That's what my song is about."

Is there anybody out there
    Who might know this little man?
Is there anybody out there
    Who can tell me who I am?

Can you tell me what my name is?
    Can you tell me where I'm from?
Was it Plymouth, York or London?
    Am I Harry, Dick or Tom?

Was I rich and was I famous,
    Was I poor, was I unknown?
Have I children and a wife somewhere,
    Or did I live alone?

Is there anybody out there
    Who might know this little man?
Is there someone, somewhere
    Who can tell me who on earth I am?

"Poor Cookee, that's the saddest song I've ever heard," said Roger, wiping a tear from his eye.

"Aye – well, that's the way the cookie crumbles," said Cookee with a chuckle. "Here, try this pirate suit on for size."

Roger cheered up at once when he saw himself in the mirror.

"That's more like it!" he shouted. "Now I look like a real pirate!"

PART III
Roger to the Rescue

Roger and Cookee waited three days
for the pirates to return, but there was
no sign of them. Not even a postcard.

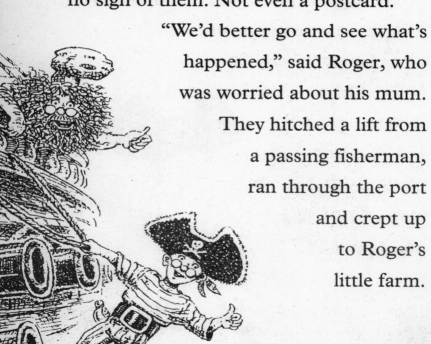

"We'd better go and see what's
happened," said Roger, who
was worried about his mum.
They hitched a lift from
a passing fisherman,
ran through the port
and crept up
to Roger's
little farm.

This is what they saw.

Roger's mum was in charge!
Smothered in swords
and pistols, she had
the pirates working
like slaves!

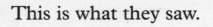

Get to work!

Roger sneaked over to Khan the Really Nasty: "Psst, Khan! What happened?"

"Jolly Roger!" said Khan with a start. "We've been captured!"

"How?" said Roger. "There are eleven of you and only one of her!"

"When we got here," said Khan, "we shut her in the house and started havin' some fun: chuckin' things around an' breakin' things up. Well, then we found some rum an' we had a party! We got drunk as lords an' fell asleep. When we woke up we was chained hand an' foot. Prisoners! Since then it's been terrible! First she made us wash! Then she put us to work and every night she chains us up in the barn!"

From across the farmyard Roger's mum screamed, "KHAN! Haven't you finished that washing-up yet, you lazy barbarian?"

"Almost done, ma'am," replied Khan
in a weedy little voice. "You'd better go!"
he hissed to Roger. "We told her we'd
press-ganged you an' she says unless we
tell her where you are she's going to
twist our ears off."

Roger crept back to Cookee and told
him the bad news. "We must help
them!" said Roger. "They'll never
escape on their own."
"Right!" said Cookee.
"But let's wait
till it's dark."

KHAN!

PART IV
The Great Escape

Just before dawn, Roger and Cookee made their move. "Follow me," whispered Roger. "There are some loose boards round the back of the barn."

Once inside, they crept up to the slumbering pirates.

"Captain!" hissed Roger.

"WHAT? Curse yer! Who be that disturbin' me beauty sleep? Oooh-arrgh!"

"It's all right," said Cookee, "he's like this every morning when I take him his Rice Krispies soaked with rum."

Roger found the keys and set the pirates free.

"Let's go," he whispered, "but don't make a sound."

They were crossing the yard when:

"KABOOOOM!!!" roared a blunderbuss over their heads.

"Get back in that barn, you hooligans!" yelled Roger's mum.

"Arrgh!" howled the captain, stepping on a rake and blacking his good eye. "Be this the end of Abdul the Skinhead…?

"To die so
young, oooh-arrgh,
in me prime!"

"Oh, come on, you
big baby!" hissed Roger.

"That's no way to talk
to yer captain!"
whimpered Abdul.
"Men have walked
the plank for less!"

"Yes, well, we'll discuss it later," said
Roger. "Meanwhile, let's get out of here!"

Through the streets the terrified pirates
ran, Roger's mum hot on their heels.
What a sight! What a to-do!
There hadn't been so much excitement
since Sir Walter Raleigh
opened the town's first
fish and chip shop!

The pirates hurled themselves into
their rowing boat and furiously set off,
heaving and lurching across the harbour.

"Come back here, you louts!"
yelled Roger's mum. "I'll teach you
to pinch my Roger!" And picking up
a wooden bucket …

… she hurled it at the
escaping pirates.
It landed with a
mighty "CLONK!"
smack bang on

Cookee's hairy head, knocking him
senseless and sending him toppling into
the water.

"MAN OVERBOARD!" shouted
Roger. "Turn the boat around!"

"No fear!"
barked Abdul. "It's
every man for himself!
Pull harder, ye dogs,
or there'll be no cocoa
in bed tonight!
Oooh-arrgh!"

"Anyway," panted Riff-raff Rafferty,
"none of us can swim."

"CAN'T SWIM!" shouted Roger.
And with these words our hero
dived into the shark-infested waters
(well, sardine-infested, actually).

At the same moment, Roger's mum
dived from the quay. They reached
Cookee just as he was going down for
the third time.

PART V
Cookee tells all!
EXCLUSIVE!

With the aid of a boat-hook Cookee
was lifted out of the water and lain
with a squelch on the quay.

He slowly opened his eyes,
removed a sardine from
his mouth, then spoke
these startling words:
"Ernestine!
Is that you? Don't
you recognize me?

It's your long-lost husband, Henry!
That bang on the nut has given me
back me memory!"

Everyone gasped.

"DAD!" shouted Roger.

"HALLELUJAH!" cried Ernestine.

Then she did something Roger had never seen in all his nine years – she smiled.

Roger was shocked.

His mum's face was … well, pretty!

Meanwhile, well away from all that
soppy nonsense, the pirates were heading
in the general direction of somewhere
a long way away from Roger's mum.

"I'd rather take me chances with a two-hundred-gun Spanish man-o-war than tackle that woman again!" roared the captain. "Next time ye press-gang a cabin boy make sure you take a look at his mum first!"

And so with a final "Oooh-arrgh!" we take our leave of the pirates of Abdul the Skinhead, and return to dry land.

PART VI
Celebration!

A party had started on the quay.
There was much singing of sea shanties
and much dancing of sailor-type jigs.

People laughed and people cried and
a rollicking good time was had by all.

Roger's dad told of his adventures
with the pirates, and Roger's mum told
of the hard times they had been through.

Roger's dad had a shave and haircut.
Without all that hair he was … well,
quite handsome!

After a cracking party, Roger and his mum and dad headed home.

"Come on," said Roger's mum. "That farm won't run itself, you know. There's work to be done!"

Roger and his dad burst out laughing. "Aye-aye, Captain!" they said. "Aye-aye!"

AUTHOR'S NOTE

You have probably noticed
some awful spelling in this book.
Sorry, but that's the only way
I can show you how pirates spoke.
(Don't let your teacher see!)